Soft Butter's Ghost

and Himself

MARTIN WADDELL

Illustrated by JAMES MAYHEW

ORCHARD BOOKS

For Jess, Kate and Tom, one dark night!
J.M

ORCHARD BOOKS
96 Leonard Street, London EC2A 4XD
Hachette Children's Books Australia
Level 17/207 Kent Street, Sydney NSW 2000
ISBN 1 84362 425 7 (hardback)
ISBN 1 84362 430 3 (paperback)
The text was first published in the form of a gift collection called *The Orchard Book of Ghostly Stories* illustrated by Sophy Williams, in Great Britain in 2000
This edition first published in hardback in 2005
First paperback publication in 2006
Text © Martin Waddell 2000
Illustrations © James Mayhew 2005
The rights of Martin Waddell to be identified as the author
and of XXXX to be identified as the illustrator of this work
have been asserted by them in accordance with the
Copyright, Designs and Patents Act, 1988.
A CIP catalogue record for this book is available
from the British Library.
1 3 5 7 9 10 8 6 4 2 (hardback)
1 3 5 7 9 10 8 6 4 2 (paperback)
Printed in Great Britain
www.wattspublishing.co.uk

CONTENTS

Soft Butter's Ghost

There was once an old farmer called Butter. He was gentle and kind and lived all by himself with a pig and a sheep and a goat that he spoiled, for he loved them too much, which is no way for a farmer to be.

"Pigs are for killing for bacon, and sheep are for shearing, and we get fine cheese from our goat!" people told him.

"Is that so?" said the farmer, and he moved the pig and the sheep and the goat into the house with himself, for they were his friends.

Everyone thought he was mad. They called him 'Soft Butter'. I don't think he was mad. I think he was lonely.

One day Soft Butter
went to the fair, and
he met a fine girl
called Miranda. She
hadn't a penny to
put to her name,
but she had
a good heart,
and she fell for
Soft Butter. She
made him feel
grand with her
hand on his
arm. She soon
had Soft Butter
bewitched with
her smile, though
that doesn't take
much with a
lonely old man.

"Will you wed?"
asked Soft Butter.
"Have you a pig?"
asked Miranda.
"I have," said Soft Butter.
"Have you a sheep?" asked Miranda.
"I have," said Soft Butter.
"Have you a goat?"
asked Miranda.

"I have," said Soft
Butter, a little surprised
that she'd asked, for
he thought she would
follow her heart,
and he knew
it was good.
"Then I'll wed!" said
Miranda, quite quickly
in case he'd think of
changing his mind.

It wasn't a trick or a scheme. She loved him. She wanted to marry Soft Butter, but she'd been told what to ask by her Aunt Clicky Tongue, and she was afraid of her auntie.

And so they were married the next market-day and Miranda went out to the farm with Soft Butter.

She made good friends with the pig and the sheep and the goat, for she was gentle and kind like Soft Butter. The pair were well met.

That should have been that, but
it wasn't.

The week after they wed, with her hat
on her head and her bag in her hand, up
the lane to the farm came Aunt Clicky
Tongue. She marched in through the
door on the two love-a-doves, without
even asking their leave.

"Here's a fine house!" said Aunt Clicky Tongue. "But the beasts would keep better out in the field!"

And she turfed out the pig and the sheep and the goat.

"Now see here…" began old Soft Butter.

"See what?" said Aunt Clicky Tongue. "See what-did-you-say?" And she gave him a look that would kill.

"Oh, never mind," said Soft Butter, turning away, for he couldn't stand up to Aunt Clicky Tongue. He was too kind and too gentle to cross her.

"There's room here for more!" said Aunt Clicky Tongue, and she sent for her cousin, old Joe, and her three spotty sisters, and two friends and their uncle with pains in his knee.

They all came up the lane to Soft Butter's Farm, and Soft Butter went down to the road and brought up their bags, for Aunt Clicky Tongue told him to do it.

"There's no room for us all!" mumbled Soft Butter.

"Then you may sleep in the barn!" said Aunt Clicky Tongue. "For these are your guests in your house, and you cannot be putting them out!"

"Auntie dear…" murmured Miranda.

"What's this? Have you something to say?" growled Aunt Clicky Tongue.

"I said nothing at all," said Miranda,

just wilting away, for she was very scared of her auntie.

The two lovey-doves set up their nest in the barn, and the house was filled with the aunt and her people. Aunt Clicky Tongue charged some of them rent, which she kept for herself so it wouldn't bother Miranda.

None of them worked, except Soft Butter and Soft Butter's wife.

It was "Butter, do this!" and "Butter, do that!" and "Butter, don't be forgetting to do things our way!" all the day from Aunt Clicky Tongue, her cousin, old Joe, her three sisters, the two friends and their uncle with pains in his knee.

It all got too much for Soft Butter. He sat in the field with the pig and the sheep and the goat and he sighed, but that didn't do him much good.

He gave up, and he died in the field with his friends.

Poor Miranda! She cried and she sobbed her heart out for Soft Butter.

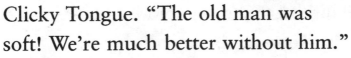

"No more of that, girl!" said her Aunt Clicky Tongue. "The old man was soft! We're much better without him."

They buried Soft Butter in the low field, for Aunt Clicky Tongue wouldn't let Miranda pay gold for a grave at the church. She told Miranda they needed their money to pay for the living.

It was a mistake, though she didn't
know it, for somehow Soft Butter was
still on the farm, just waiting for
something to waken his heart.

Now there was no one to do any
work round the place but Miranda.
She did what she was bid by her Aunt
Clicky Tongue, slaving all day to
care for the rest but, oh dear! she
was missing Soft Butter.

The poor girl hid in the
low field by the grave
and she grieved for
Soft Butter, with the
pig and the sheep
and the goat, who
were sorely put
out. No one else
knew she was sad,
and no one else cared.

But something stirred in the field,
wakened by the tears that the girl shed
for Soft Butter.

The very next night, with the daylight
growing dim, there was a stir in the
yard. The two friends and their uncle
with pains in the knee all ran to look,
though the uncle ran slowly because of
his pains.

There was a ghost in the yard, white as a sheet and gliding about. There was no moaning and groaning or clanging of chains, for he wasn't that kind of ghost.

"A g-g-ghost!" cried the uncle with pains.

"Never mind that," said the pig, looking over the fence. "Sure, it's only the ghost of our friend the farmer, Soft Butter!"

But the two friends and the uncle with pains paid no heed to a pig (even a pig who could talk), for they knew a ghost when they saw one. They thought it would eat them alive!

"AHHHHHHHHH!" screamed the two friends and the uncle with pains in his knee. They were scared stiff by the ghost-in-the-yard and they ran off over the fields in their nightclothes. The uncle ran fastest of all getting out, and jumped highest of all getting over the gate, so it seems he was cured of the pains in his knee.

They never came back to Soft Butter's Farm. Nobody minded, and nobody missed them, though Aunt Clicky Tongue thought she would miss the rent.

The next night was worse! There was the ghost in the front room where the three spotty sisters slept on the floor, and old Cousin Joe had the sofa. The ghost hovered about above them and wakened them up. It was gentle and kind and would do them no harm, but they didn't know that. They were frightened.

"Never mind that!" said the sheep, looking in at the window. "It's only the ghost of our friend the farmer, Soft Butter."

The three spotty sisters and old Cousin Joe paid no heed to the sheep, for they didn't believe that they had heard a sheep talking, but they knew very well that they'd seen a ghost...

They fled out of the house, down the lane, screaming their heads off. They never came back to Soft Butter's Farm. Nobody minded, and nobody missed them.

Next night came, and there was the ghost in Aunt Clicky Tongue's room.

Something was drifting about by the bed, over her head. It was too much for Aunt Clicky Tongue! She stuck her hat on her head, and belted right out of the house down the lane.

The goat
watched her go,
but he didn't say
anything. He was
a wise goat
for a goat, and he
wanted her out of the
way! So he didn't say
it was only the ghost of his
friend the farmer, Soft Butter,
in case she believed him and stayed.

Aunt Clicky Tongue never came back
to Soft Butter's farm, not even to pick
up her teeth which she'd left in the glass,
nor the rent money she'd kept from
Miranda. The loss of the teeth put an
end to their clicking, and the loss of
the money just served her right!

The last night of all there was no one
to scare, for no one was there but
Miranda, and Soft Butter's ghost...there
in the glow by the fire, with the pig and
the sheep and the wise goat, fetched in
from the field. They were together again
for a while. It was a gentle sweet time
for them all, being together again. Then
Soft Butter's ghost faded away in the
firelight, at home, with his friends,

and that was the end of Soft Butter.

But it wasn't the end of Miranda. She stayed on the farm, with the pig and the sheep and the goat. The love in their hearts for Soft Butter helped her to live out her life. When she died she was buried right there in the low field, beside her Soft Butter... And so were the pig and the sheep and the goat when they died in their turn.

They're all ghosts now, out in the field,
Soft Butter, Miranda, the pig and the
sheep and the goat. They're still there
together haunting the field, the ghosts
of Soft Butter, Miranda, the pig and
the sheep and the goat.

Himself

Dan Morgan worked all alone on his farm so he talked to Himself as he dug in the fields.

"We're best by ourselves," Dan told Himself.

"Maybe we are," said Himself.

One day, down Dan's lane, came
a pretty young girl, stepping light as a
bird; her name was Chrissy. She looked
at Dan and she liked what she saw:
a sturdy young man who had fields of
his own that he worked all alone.

"Speak to her, man, if you must!"
said Himself. "Get her out of your head,
so we can get on with our work."

"Good morning, young lady!" said
Dan, very bravely.

Chrissy was
too shy to speak,
although she felt
pleased that Dan
called her a lady.
She blushed red
and walked on.

"I spoke, and
she didn't, and that
leaves me looking a fool!"
Dan told Himself. "She's too fine a
lady to speak to a man that works rough
in the fields."

"You could spruce yourself up,"
suggested Himself. "Put a rose in your
hat and you'll be a new Dan."

"That's all very well," Dan told
Himself. "But what about you?"

"I'll stay where I am, hidden inside
you, where she can't see," said Himself.

The next day Dan went to the fair
with a rose in his hat and Chrissy was
there in her Sunday-best clothes, so
she'd look like a lady for Dan. They met
and they stopped for a chat, and this led
to that, greatly delighting them both.
Chrissy rode home in the cart with her
father, to save her fine shoes, which she
held on her lap. She had only the one
pair, so she needed to save them for
being with Dan.

And so it went on as you'd guess. No
work was done in Dan's fields, but the
young couple met every day, and they
talked and they walked, and Dan took
her dancing at Breen's. That night his
Chrissy gave him a kiss,
and the kiss set poor
Dan in a whirl.

"Am I sick in
the head?" Dan
asked Himself.

"I was
thinking the same
thing myself," said
Himself. "But there's no
help for it the way you are now.
Leave the weeds to get on with growing,
for it's time that you asked for her hand!"

That shook Dan to the roots of
his boots.

"She'd never have me," Dan told Himself.

"She'll never have you if you don't ask!" said Himself. "What I think is this: she's seen the new Dan and she likes him. If he asks her, she'll have him, so long as she doesn't see me."

"And what will we do about you?" Dan asked Himself. "I'll stay hidden inside the new Dan," said Himself. "You don't need the rough honest man when you're doing your wooing. Save that man for the work in the fields."

"I'll give it a go,"
Dan told Himself
and he put on his
suit and went off to
speak to her father.
When Dan came back
he was glowing for he
had his bride promised, and three
good fields of land that went with her.

Well, they were married, and Chrissy
came to the farm, to live there with Dan
and Himself.

"She'll want changes made," Dan
told Himself. "This house is no place for
a lady like Chrissy!"

"Maybe the place needed changing!"
Himself replied. "Get on and do it, never
mind about me!"

"Just you stay inside, and I'll do it,"
said Dan.

Dan set about changing the place the very first day Chrissy was there. He bought her a fine settle chair that was fit for a lady to sit on, and a vase full of flowers she could look at.

"I'll do my turn in the fields," Chrissy told Dan, and she rolled up her sleeves, and took hold of the spade. She was a strong girl and she knew she should work with her man, like any girl would when she married a farmer.

"My wife should sit by the fire," replied Dan, and he took the spade from her and he sent her inside, for he knew that he'd married a pretty young girl and he thought she'd expect him to spoil her.

Chrissy had nothing to do but look at the flowers in the vase, and she soon tired of that, so she thought she'd chop wood and tell Dan the fairies had done it.

Dan caught her out on her way to the yard with the hatchet.

"That's no job for a lady like you," Dan scolded Chrissy. "You leave that alone, Chrissy dear. You sit in my house and look pretty!" And he sent Chrissy back to her seat by the fire.

"I did that right," Dan told Himself. "What about chopping the wood?" said Himself, but Dan didn't listen. He was too busy planning how he'd please his Chrissy to think about work that had to be done.

"It's time I got out," muttered Himself, who was afraid he might smother and die inside Dan.

"You'll stay where you are!" replied Dan. "I don't want her to see you."

Chrissy sat by the fire and thought of the Dan that she'd seen in the field the very first day that she passed. Somehow the Dan that she'd married was different. She twiddled her thumbs and got bored. She loved Dan and wanted to please him, but how could she be the lady Dan wanted for all of the rest of her life?

She thought she'd nip up and see
to the pigs.

Dan caught her at it, of course.

"I married a lady and that's what
you'll be!" Dan shouted at Chrissy, and
he ordered her back to the house.

That made Chrissy cross, but Dan
wouldn't listen. He stormed out of the
house, and left Chrissy to weep by
the fire.

"You're to blame," Dan told Himself.
"It takes a rough man from the field to
bring a lady to tears, and you've popped
out of me and you've done it!"

"And who am I but you?"
grumbled Himself.

"I've changed," said
Dan. "A man has to
change when he
marries a lady."

"I don't know
how to change,"
said Himself, and
he twisted and turned
inside Dan, trying
hard to get out,
though Dan wouldn't let him.

It was too much for Dan. Dan knew
that Himself couldn't change, deep inside,
so Dan made a plan to be rid of Himself.

He rented a stone house on the far side of the hill. That way he could do the rough work in his fields with Himself without being seen by his wife.

"Don't tell a soul about the new house," Dan warned Chrissy, for he didn't want word to get round to Himself. He thought he could slip off to the new house without Himself knowing.

That night they put all their things in the cart and went off in the dark like two mice on the flit. Of course, it thundered and poured as they went the long road.

"We'll start a new life," Dan told his wife as they huddled together on top of the cart. "I'll be the man with the rose in his hat, and you'll be the fine lady I married."

"Well, maybe," Chrissy said, biting her lip. She was scared he would guess that she wasn't a lady, for she loved her Dan and she wanted to please him.

By midnight they were at the new house built of stone, wet through and shivering, but glad in their hearts, for they were young and in love and just married.

Dan opened the door with the new key, pleased as punch to be in a new house that he'd share with his wife.

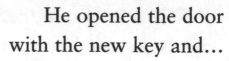 He opened the door
with the new key and...

There was Himself by the fire.

"What took you so long on the road?"
said Himself.

Dan gave a roar.

Chrissy heard him shout and she
thought Dan was killed so she ran into
the house through the door and...

And there was her Dan...kicking
Himself around the room.

AND...

Chrissy saw Himself, for the very first time.

"Stop kicking that man this minute!" said Chrissy to Dan.

Himself was all mud from the work in the fields but Chrissy thought he was nice, and he had a look of her Dan, although he had no rose in his hat.

The more she looked at Himself, the more she saw Dan!

"Who is this poor man?" she asked Dan. "Who is this poor man you've been kicking?"

"Well...Himself is myself, the way I really am," confessed Dan, blushing red. "I've tried to get rid of Himself, for he's just a rough man that works in the fields and not good enough to be married to you."

"Now I see how it is," Chrissy said with a smile. "But wait till I show you my secret!" and she opened the door and called to someone she'd left crying there, out in the cold.

"Here's someone just like Himself," she told Dan. "Someone I've kept hidden from you."

And in from the dark walked...

Herself.

And then something strange happened.

There were four in the room but... the four became two...

Dan and Chrissy.

More about the Stories...

These stories are all my own work, but they are meant to sound and feel like the stories told by a Seancaiti, the gaelic word for a storyteller.

Imagine the loneliness of a tiny cottage on a bog road, the pitch darkness outside, the firelight and the smells of the turf. There were hidden meanings in the old stories, for those who had learned how to listen!

Martin Waddell

SOFT BUTTER'S GHOST

Many a big man is meek and mild and accommodating in his soul, and lets the world run rings round him. In Ireland we would call such a man "soft as butter", and it was this phrase that led me to write this story of a gentle ghost. The names in the story are part of the game: Aunt Clicky Tongue and Soft Butter and the lovely Miranda. I would have to admit that I haven't met many Irish country girls called Miranda, but the name seemed right, and it is my story so I used it.

HIMSELF

The first ghostly story I wrote was *Himself*. Himself is not a ghost-from-the-grave ghost, bloodless bones and sightless eye-sockets, the stuff of nightmares, but a ghost of quite another kind, a ghost from within, a ghost that everyone born has to live with. I don't know how I came to write that story. It is like nothing I have written before and it just came.

I wrote this story partly with the Irish storyteller Liz Weir in mind. I was thinking how she would enjoy the teasing play with the word "himself" and the mischief of the whole thing. It felt great to be able to do a story that was at once light and funny, but at the same time had a very serious edge to it. Like Dan, we all put roses in our hats and present the outside world with what we hope is an acceptable pattern of behaviour, but what happens if this puts us at odds with the feelings of the real Dan inside?